Tea in Pajamas

Tea in Pajamas

Rachel Tey

WITHDRAWN

Marshall Cavendish
Editions

First published in 2015 by Rachel Tey
This edition published in 2018 by Marshall Cavendish Editions
An imprint of Marshall Cavendish International

A member of the
Times Publishing Group

Other Marshall Cavendish Offices:
Marshall Cavendish Corporation. 99 White Plains Road, Tarrytown NY
10591-9001, USA • Marshall Cavendish International (Thailand) Co Ltd.
253 Asoke, 12th Flr, Sukhumvit 21 Road, Klongtoey Nua, Wattana,
Bangkok 10110, Thailand • Marshall Cavendish (Malaysia) Sdn Bhd,
Times Subang, Lot 46, Subang Hi-Tech Industrial Park, Batu Tiga, 40000
Shah Alam, Selangor Darul Ehsan, Malaysia

Marshall Cavendish is a registered trademark of Times Publishing Limited

National Library Board, Singapore Cataloguing-in-Publication Data

Name(s): Tey, Rachel, 1980- author.
Title: Tea in pajamas / Rachel Tey.
Description: Singapore : Marshall Cavendish Editions, 2018.
Identifier(s): OCN 1050083279 | ISBN 978-981-48-2885-7 (paperback)
Subject(s): LCSH: Hope--Juvenile fiction. | Girls--Juvenile fiction. | Magic
--Juvenile fiction. | Art--Juvenile fiction. | Music--Juvenile fiction.
Classification: DDC S823--dc23

Printed in Singapore

Illustrations on front cover and inside pages by Joseph Tey

To
Ignacia

Tick Tock, Tick Tock...

On Wednesday afternoon at 3 o'clock, Belle Marie sat down for tea. Except she had never been fond of tea. Instead, she fancied coffee, served from a teapot and drunk from a teacup. Into the delicious dark brew she added a spoonful of sugar and dribbled whirls of fresh milk. And though she liked the smell of her mother's freshly baked butter scones, Belle preferred the soft, flaky texture of croissants.

There was yet another important component of teatime – she had to be in pajamas. If you thought it odd that at exactly 3 o'clock every Wednesday, eleven-year-old, auburn-haired Belle from the tiny town of Michelmont would come home from school, change into night clothes and savor croissants and coffee at teatime, you shared the sentiments of her parents, Mr and Mrs Marie, and her older brother, Éric. Unlike her, they were perfectly content with buttered raisin scones, washed down nicely with cups of Earl Grey. They also never wore pajamas in the afternoon or went about barefoot.

To all this, Belle paid little attention, for there were more pressing matters at hand. Unbeknownst to her family (and the rest of the world), a midweek tea session at home in sleepwear was no ordinary affair. It was the crucial step to unlocking the doors and stepping into a wondrous place of magic – Belzerac.

7, 6, 5, 4, 3, 2, 1 ... Belle finished the last of her croissant and put down her teacup. She dusted the flaky pastry crumbs off her striped cotton pajamas and smoothed down her mane of ginger curls. "I'm ready now," she whispered, "let's go."

It always happened quickly from that point. The last thing she remembered hearing was Éric asking, "What's for tea?"

Easy as Pie

"You have exactly one hour left!" bellowed Monsieur DuPorc through the loudhailer. "If you haven't already started on your pie filling, now would be a good time!" The talking pig was presiding over the day's pie-making competition as both host and judge. He also happened to be the mayor of Belzerac. Monsieur DuPorc was certainly smartly dressed for the occasion. Clad in a powder blue suit, he would have looked very handsome were he not perspiring so profusely from the unrelenting heat of the afternoon sun.

Pie filling? Belle opened her eyes and saw that she was standing behind a table, alongside some familiar faces, and some others she was only seeing for the first time. Scattered haphazardly in front of her was a weighing scale, a mixing bowl, flour, sugar, salt, a single vanilla pod, butter cubes on a glass dish, a jug of milk, a lemon, and a large basket of whole pitted cherries in the most vivid of shade of red. She also saw that she had on a blue-and-white gingham apron over her pajamas, the same one donned by the other contestants around her.

Did she have enough time to finish? Belle took a moment to gather her thoughts. Her pie dough had been formed and rolled into two beige spheres – she now had to flatten each ball into a disc, a job for the rolling pin she found clutched in her flour-specked hands. She did this quickly so she could move on to her filling. Into her mixing bowl went the sugar and a pinch of salt, followed by the cherries, seeds from the vanilla pod, and the juice of half the lemon. As she stirred the pretty ruby mixture with her wooden spoon and breathed in the syrupy scent of vanilla, she couldn't help but notice the empty table to her right where it looked as if another contestant should have been. "Tess Brown" read the name on the place card. *Tess! Where could she be?*

Tess and Belle were best friends and classmates in the same elementary school. They also lived in the same neighborhood, rode the school bus together and between them, there were no secrets. Their shared discovery of the extraordinary village of Belzerac via the passage of Tea in Pajamas laid the foundation for many a colorful and exciting experience away from their hometown of Michelmont — an adventure they each swore never to embark on without the other. They had decided that at 3 o'clock after school every Wednesday, they would change into their pajamas and sit for tea in their respective homes.

And without fail, the girls would show up together in Belzerac. This Wednesday should not have been any different, but strangely, Tess was nowhere to be seen.

"Half an hour to go!" The booming voice of Monsieur DuPorc jolted Belle back to her present task at hand. Quickly, she laid part of her dough at the bottom of the pie dish, trimmed away the excess, then poured the cherry filling over. Next, she arranged strips of dough in a crisscross fashion over the glistening crimson mixture, and sealed the edges of her pie with her fingertips. In swift but steady motions, Belle brushed her pie lightly with milk before the final flourish — a modest sprinkling of sugar.

"FIFTEEN MINUTES!"

By this time, most contestants already had their pies in the oven — any further delay would be cutting it too close. Pie in hand, Belle made large strides across the open green field to the enormous common oven where her pastry joined the rest of the contending creations, some quite handsome and others not quite so. *Phew!*

"I must say you stand a mighty good chance of winning. I hear Monsieur and Madame DuPorc love cherries." Belle turned to see Cheesy Bear, his apron still on and paws in oven mitts which he looked to have no intention of removing. "But to have done a cherry pie would just have been taking the easy way out. Everyone knows I love a good challenge," he continued.

Cheesy Bear was the first friend Belle had made in Belzerac when she first turned up two years ago, bewildered and petrified. Until then, she had never traveled outside Michelmont, so to have found herself amid talking animals in an idyllic setting without cars or tall buildings was astonishing to say the least. Having caught sight of a red-haired, pajama-clad girl standing in his rose garden, Cheesy

Bear had invited the visibly shaken Belle into his cottage and soothed her frazzled nerves over a plate of cheese nibblets and a glass of warm milk. They then spent the afternoon chatting away, until the sun's receding rays signaled the point at which Belle was (and would subsequently always be) brought back to the kitchen table of her Michelmont home.

On her next visit, Belle brought with her a hitherto unconvinced Tess, and Cheesy wasted no time introducing them to the company of fellow Belzeracians, Monsieur and Madame DuPorc. Belle and Tess never knew what magical adventures awaited them each Wednesday afternoon in Belzerac. Up until then, they had, with their new friends, canoed down the Doreine (a glittering river that cut through the rolling fields and meandered beyond the distant mountains), explored mysterious caves, and enjoyed lazy picnics in the warm sunshine. Today's activity was a cinch for Belle, for she was a naturally gifted baker, though she wasn't sure if she was good enough to win a competition.

"Cheesy!" she exclaimed, reaching over to lock her furry friend in a tight embrace. "It's so good to see you again. I've missed you." That was true. To Belle, the other six days of the week away from Belzerac always felt like an eternity — particularly of late, since she had been feeling increasingly bored and restless with her life in Michelmont.

"Come on, let's take a breather before they announce the results," she said, taking the bear's oven-mitt-clad paw and leading him to a shady spot under a large elm tree. The DuPorcs, who were the organizers and judges of Belzerac's annual pie-making contest, were busy tasting pies and deciding on the winner. Each year, the champion was awarded a generous supply of butter, along with a much-coveted golden trophy, fashioned in the likeness of a rolling pin.

"What are your general thoughts on cheese as a pie filling?" Cheesy persisted, finally removing his apron and laying it on the grass for them to sit on. "I wanted to go for peaches as they are in season, but a savory pie is so much more flavorful." They rested, his thoughts on pastries and hers on her missing best friend.

"By the way, where's Tess?" Cheesy asked, as if having read her mind. At this mention, Belle felt a knot in her stomach. Since they started on Tea in Pajamas, Tess had never failed to turn up.

"I'm not sure, to be honest," she replied. "She should be here by now."

Cheesy Bear placed a reassuring paw on Belle's shoulder. "I'm sure she's alright," he said. "I suppose she forgot or is just a little delayed ... had to run a few errands and will be here soon."

"Unless ..." someone interjected in a low voice.

"Unless what?" Belle asked, turning to face Monsieur DuPorc, who had come to join them under the elm tree. Studying his grave expression, she almost dreaded to hear the answer.

"The Musicians," he said, matter-of-factly. "They may have something to do with a number of cases in which Belzeracians went mysteriously missing." He paused, studying Belle's quizzical expression. "Their music is believed to be so beautiful and beguiling, it entices the listener to seek its origin ... and thence, disappear into oblivion."

Belle could feel an unsettling mix of impatience and skepticism welling up inside her. It was easier to accept that her best friend had let their weekly Tea in Pajamas ritual slip her mind and was presently home in Michelmont, than to imagine she could be in the company of these mysterious Musicians.

"Well, technically, these have all been

third-party accounts and cautionary tales,"
Cheesy Bear chimed in, folding his burly
arms. "However, some have spoken of a
certain Monsieur L'Arbre who helps the
lost find their way back home. Perhaps
he could tell you where Tess is."

"Who is this Monsieur L'Arbre?" Belle
asked, anxious for answers.

Monsieur DuPorc held up his right front
trotter to pause the conversation and
indicate that he had to return to the judges'
bench to announce the results of the pie
contest. She watched as he hurried back
to the makeshift podium and retrieved
his loudhailer.

"Contestants, if you would all gather
back here, please, for the results!"

It was prize-giving time. Belle could
not help but marvel at the three rolling-
pin-shaped trophies set before everyone.
Arranged in descending order of height,
they gleamed so brightly it hurt to even
look at them.

The next twenty minutes or so went by in a blur. There was much clapping and many happy gasps from the crowd as names were called out and speeches were made. Belle could only presume she wasn't among the top three since no one was as much as looking in her direction. Instead, her thoughts drifted to the last time she had seen her best friend.

They had both taken the school bus home earlier that day, and Belle had been the first to alight. Oddly enough, neither of them had spoken of Belzerac, their conversation instead centering on the new boy in class, Julien, whose crop of spiky, seemingly gravity-defying blond hair had drawn manifold guffaws from the other children.

"Do you suppose he puts something in it to make it stand?" Tess had wondered aloud. The rest of the journey home went by uneventfully and when the bus pulled up in front of Belle's home, the girls said their usual goodbyes.

Maybe I should have reminded her about Tea in Pajamas, she thought, regretfully. For now, though, there was the question of Monsieur L'Arbre.

"He is said to be a 2,000-year-old tree that resides in the Sapphire Forest. And like a lighthouse, he guides lost travelers back to safety," said Monsieur DuPorc in answer to Belle's burning question. Their conversation had resumed now that the prize-giving ceremony was over and the crowd had dispersed. A strong buttery smell continued to linger in the air.

Belle felt herself cheering to the prospect of meeting this formidable, magical tree. "Let's go to him — he'll know for sure what happened to Tess. I just hope it's not too late."

"Hold on, there's a catch. Actually two," Cheesy Bear cut in, his lips now pursed and brows knitted in a tight frown. "As Monsieur DuPorc said, he resides in the Sapphire Forest — a dark and dangerous place. Only half of those who have ever ventured in have made it back unscathed, while the rest remain unaccounted for."

"And the Musicians may have something to do with that," added Madame DuPorc.

They were right. It wasn't going to be easy. Belle looked down at her bare feet, feeling the cold, damp grass beneath her soles. *How am I supposed to trek through the woods, fraught with obstacles and menacing characters, without any shoes?* she wondered.

"Don't be discouraged, there is hope yet," said Madame DuPorc, reaching over to lock Belle in a motherly embrace. "Why, it's almost sunset. You'll soon return to Michelmont and find out for certain if Tess is home."

"Yes, exactly," agreed Cheesy Bear. "We'll look out for her here until your return next Wednesday, by which time I'm positive she would've shown up on either side. If not, we can both go into Sapphire Forest to find Monsieur L'Arbre."

"Count us in," echoed the DuPorcs, clearly in support of Cheesy's plan.

"Thank you," Belle said, holding back grateful tears. "I couldn't ask for better mates."

Together, they sat under the old elm tree, till the last vestiges of daylight faded into the rusty glow of evening. Any time now, she would be back in Michelmont.

Belle closed her eyes, basking in the promise of a new day.

Julien Hedgehog

Julien had never understood why the hairs on his head perpetually stood on end as if willed to do so by an inexplicable force of nature. He'd tried everything — washing it up to five times a day, slicking on his father's hair gel, combing, brushing, even arranging his pillows into a boxed formation around his head as he slept — but the result was always the same. The reflection in the mirror consistently showed a pale young lad with linear, sandy spikes for hair.

One time, his mother had the barber shear it down to a uniform one-inch height, but as if in protest, the bristles grew back taller, thicker, and thornier within a week.

Actually, Julien had come to accept and even embrace this unique feature about himself. If anything, it drew attention away from his rather freckly face, another aspect of his appearance he could do without if he so had the choice. However, this was not to say he disliked everything about himself— in fact, he was happy with his eyes, slightly close-set but in the most intriguing shade of stormy gray.

He was also proud of his photographic memory— once an image, sound, or object was imprinted in his mind, he possessed the unique ability to recall all of it with amazing precision. This gift earned him such good grades that he wasn't short of offers from schools when his family relocated from Suffingshire to Michelmont following his father's new job posting. Eventually, Julien was enrolled in Lutetia Elementary School for Boys and Girls.

Julien Hedgehog. He was not new to nicknames – in his former school, he had been called everything from Daggerhead to Spiky Spud – he just hadn't expected to be given a label on his first day at Lutetia.

It began innocently enough during attendance-taking. Mrs Wilson was doing the routine roll call and by the time she got to his name, it was just par for the course.

"We have a new student joining our class," she said, smiling in his direction. "Stand up, Mr Edgehawk."

The subsequent chortles that filled the classroom left Julien red-faced. He rose from his seat amidst a chorus of taunts that only grew louder as more joined in.

"HEDGEHOG! HEDGEHOG! HEDGEHOG!"

He sighed. Why did human beings have to be so predictable?

Julien looked down at his lunch tray and felt quite pleased with the variety of offerings available at Lutetia. If anything, his chicken casserole with green beans and raspberry pudding dessert looked much more appetizing than the usual peas-and-mash or tuna fish sandwiches served back at his old school. Now if he could just find a quiet, inconspicuous spot to enjoy his meal undisturbed.

Most of the tables were already occupied by well-established cliques or study groups deep in discussions in between mouthfuls of lunch. Julien scanned the cafeteria for any solitary diners whom he could only hope would share a table with him. There were several tables he spotted— at one was seated a rather overweight boy who almost took up the entire bench, and at another rested a tired, bespectacled girl so deep in slumber it would have been cruel to awaken her with the sounds of his chewing.

Finally, Julien's eyes rested on a sullen-looking redhead, a girl he recognized as his classmate. He struggled to recall her name — was it Bella? Hopefully, she wouldn't refuse him a seat. "Umm ... hi, we're in the same class ... I was wondering ..."

The girl looked up, still stirring her mug of hot cocoa with a silver teaspoon. The corners of her mouth turned upward to form a faint smile and he noticed that she had very pretty green eyes. "Julien Edgehawk, isn't it? I'm Belle Marie. Sit down if you like."

"Oh. Thanks," he mumbled, caught offguard by her affability. While he hadn't expected her to wave him away dismissively, neither had he foreseen such a show of courtesy, especially from such a striking girl. His mother had always said to watch out for the most beautiful ones – they had the worst manners – and examples at his previous school only proved as much. He felt a distinct uneasiness.

Belle Marie was not eating. Her chicken casserole was untouched and she was instead pushing the green beans around her plate with her fork, mopping up all traces of gravy in the process. Her pudding looked likely to join the rest of her uneaten lunch.

"Aren't you going to have something?" he finally asked. He was by now getting to the end of his meal but she had only taken two sips of her hot chocolate. For her earlier show of friendliness that stood in stark contrast to the rest of his name-calling classmates, he felt obliged to make some outward display of concern. "Don't you think you might get hungry later?"

"I might," she said, taking a small bite of her casserole. "It's just that I usually eat with Tess and I'm worried about her."

Tess. That name sounded familiar. Julien now called to mind another classmate: a raven-haired girl who always wore a blue headband. Seeing them practically joined at the hip in class and on the school bus, he should have deduced that they were close. It then occurred to him that he himself hadn't seen Tess at class for almost a week.

"Is she ill?" he asked, thinking it might explain Belle's present glum disposition. He moved on quickly to his dessert. English class was due to start in about ten minutes and he loathed being late.

"She isn't," she replied, after a short pause. "Just missing."

Missing? Now that sounded serious. Back in Suffingshire where he came from, Julien had heard his share of horror stories about children who'd disappeared without a trace, never to be found. In addition, there was talk of kidnappers prowling the streets for easy victims — unsuspecting schoolchildren. Mr and Mrs Edgehawk were naturally very protective over their four sons. Julien (the youngest) and his brothers were taught never to wander off on their own or speak to strangers. He supposed the same dangers lurked in Michelmont.

"The thing is," Belle went on, "she's not really missing. I mean she *is*, but not *here*."

The obvious irony of what he just heard puzzled him. "Do you mean to say she's lost, but you have some idea where she might be?"

Belle nodded. Then, unexpectedly, she reached across the table to grab his hand. Julien froze. Apart from his mother, no other girl had ever touched him.

"What are you doing next Wednesday after school?" Her soft, raspy voice brought him back to the present moment. "Also, can you keep a secret?" she asked, her gaze fixed intently on him.

"Sure, but what—"

"*Promise* first not to tell."

Her palms were oh so cold. "OK ... I won't tell," he conceded.

"It's a hideaway of sorts. Only Tess and I know how to get there."

"Then what's stopping you from going there and bringing her back?" he asked.

"It isn't so simple. I don't know her exact location but I'm going to find out where she is. I just thought I could benefit from a little assistance."

At this juncture, Julien realized this was a direct appeal to his sense of chivalry and valor. How would he respond to the first friend he ever made at Lutetia Elementary, even if it was only because she needed his help?

The bell rang, signaling the end of lunch. Now was not the time to tarry, nor for indecision. Belle was still looking at him, her emerald green eyes wide with hope. Already he knew he didn't have the heart to disappoint her.

"Alright, tell me how I can get there too."

Flights of Fancy

Belle couldn't exactly remember when and how she discovered Tea in Pajamas. Growing up, she was no stranger to imaginative play. At the age of three, she often found herself in her father's study, pouring over piles of books pulled off their shelves. Despite not yet recognizing words, and no matter their content, these volumes and their pages were the perfect stage props in her little narrations of enchanted tales of magical faraway lands and mystical creatures. When family and friends came over, she enjoyed giving colorful storytelling performances, and they indulged her flights of literary fancy.

On her fifth birthday, she was gifted with a brand new piano and ensuing piano lessons, and she took to music like a fish to water, mastering the instrument effortlessly. But to the chagrin of her teacher and parents, Belle eschewed convention, often improvising on her pieces and scales. At one point, she was only willing to play major keys on some days of the week and minor keys on others, convinced that every day had its particular "sound." This quirkiness did not sit well with her teachers (a total of five in succession), and she never made it past the Grade 3 examinations. The piano now sat quietly in the corner of her music room by a large window overlooking the garden.

However, a year later, things took a more encouraging turn when Belle was introduced to art. Aided by painting lessons from Miss Brady, a family friend, Belle's vivid imagination was transferred onto canvas in the manner of still life, followed by landscapes, then portraits, and back to landscapes again. With techniques mastered from formal instruction, she became particularly fond of painting nature in rich, earthy colors. Encouraged by her precocious talent, Miss Brady entered her in a string of competitions, and Belle went on to bag numerous awards and accolades.

Now, Belle's interest in painting had waned somewhat – she no longer took lessons from Miss Brady, nor did she take part in contests to add to her trophy cabinet. In fact, since Tea in Pajamas, many things in her life had taken secondary importance, the hours and days simply a build-up to Wednesday afternoons in Belzerac.

Just a week before Tess's disappearance, she had chanced upon some of her old artwork in the attic while rummaging for a coat. Not having seen her paintings in a while, Belle had been struck by how much they resembled scenes from Belzerac, down to its river banks, mountains, and deciduous trees.

How could I have had any impression of the place back then? she had wondered. After all, these were painted long before she came to discover Tea in Pajamas, and all that lay beyond.

Magic

"**D**o you believe in magic, Julien?" Belle was lying prone on the grass, propped up by her elbows. They had decided to skip the school bus and go for a walk after the day's lessons. Armed with chicken sandwiches and bottled juice saved from lunch, they stopped to rest their weary feet in a small open meadow behind the train station.

"Why do you ask?"

It was hard to see her expression from where he sat (adjacent and not facing) but she soon turned to lie on her back, looking straight up at the clouds. Who could guess the thoughts running through the mind of this intriguing girl he was just getting to know? With a head of tousled red tendrils that framed her delicate heart-shaped face, she reminded him of a fairy character from a children's book. And those emerald eyes, like rare green jewels, transfixed and confounded him at the same time. She seemed so preoccupied with the idea of secrets and magic, so convinced of their place in her life, yet Julien was the sort to be unnerved about suspending rational belief, even if in the name of friendship.

As if clued in to his curiosity, Belle reached into her canvas knapsack and pulled out a ratty notepad. It was ragged around the edges and heavily annotated.

"Is that your journal?" he asked, as she rummaged for a pen.

"It's not dreamy prose and insightful musings if that's what you're asking," she said matter-of-factly. "More like a log book of what I did and what transpired each time Tess and I went to Belzerac."

"I've never heard of Belzerac."

"Of course you haven't – you don't believe in magic."

Was it that obvious? He thought hard for a response, but Belle was indifferent.

"Here, take this." She tore out a page from her notepad and handed it to him. It read:

Wednesday afternoon,
3 o'clock, your home.
Sit down to have tea in
your pajamas. No shoes.

"Just follow the instructions on the note," she said plainly. "It gets you to Belzerac, where we'll meet and go find Tess."

It was already Tuesday. "That's tomorrow," he muttered, staring at the slip of paper.

"Uh huh, but it wouldn't work unless you really *believe* it, so please try to." She got to her feet, dusting stray grass and wildflowers off her school uniform. "And since we only have about a day until then, you have to start believing right now."

Julien tried to visualize the bizarre picture of his barefoot, pajama-clad self sitting down to have tea at home. He would never hear the end of it from his brothers. He didn't even have a teatime habit.

"Come on, we'd better get ourselves home," she said, pulling him to his feet. "Long day tomorrow."

Into the Woods

MISSION: RESCUE TESS

We're all sitting around Cheesy's dining table in his very charming cottage as he packs a large picnic basket for our trip into the Sapphire Forest. Who knows how long the whole journey there and back will take, but he isn't leaving anything to chance. I doubt there's any room left for that roast chicken he's yet to remove from the oven. Julien is still wearing that expression of complete disbelief on his face, and unable to utter anything beyond "yes" and "no." I hope I don't regret asking him along, and he doesn't turn out to be more of a hindrance than help. Anyway, we're now quite ready to set off any minute! Roll call: Julien, me, Cheesy Bear, Monsieur and Madame DuPorc. Everybody's here. Off we go!

※

We're in the Sapphire Forest, can hardly believe it. Having a brief respite. We're all pretty tired from the journey. The glittering blue leaves are so beautiful, but after trudging along for what's felt like forever, the forest has mostly lost its charm. Everything's just bathed in BLUE, and I can't tell what's grass or dirt. We're all hungry. The food we packed is almost all gone, and the DuPorcs think it best that we turn back at the first hint of sunset. That shouldn't be long from now, but Cheesy is confident the day will hold out until we find Monsieur L'Arbre. For my part, I'm pretty excited about meeting him/it, supposing he/it is even real. Must remain open-minded and hopeful.

Cheesy's just given the signal. Time to get moving. Wait, what is Julien doing? Is he SLEEPING? Well, he IS wearing his pajamas ...

Cheesy Bear and the DuPorcs have made the call to turn back, much to my dismay. I'm scribbling this while Julien is assuring everybody that with his photographic memory he'll definitely remember the way in and out. The blue light of the forest is now darkening into a deep violet. I don't quite know how to describe it, but the atmosphere feels ominous and rather foreboding. At least this forest has decent taste in music. It sounds like Mélodie by C.W. Gluck, inspired by the tragic Greek tale of Orpheus and Eurydice. I love this piece of classical music. But why does it feel like I'm hearing it for the first time? Hold on ... why is music playing in the forest?

What in the world?

Follow the Music

They had stepped into a pastoral paradise. Everywhere Belle looked, she saw a vast expanse of grass and trees. The wind felt like a giant hand combing its fingers tenderly through her scarlet curls and the air was heavily perfumed by the scent of lilacs. Gazing ahead, she could see nothing beyond rolling meadows that stretched into an infinity of green and sky. Gluck's *Mélodie* was still playing, but more softly, as if from a distance.

"Do you hear it too?" Julien asked.

So she wasn't alone or dreaming. Suddenly aware of the exuberance of her surroundings, she realized they were no longer in the Sapphire Forest. Far away from it, even.

"Yes, I do," she replied. "What time is it?"

He looked down at a spot on his wrist where his watch would have sat. "I ... I didn't wear a watch today."

"Why not?"

"Who wears one with their pajamas? Why didn't you wear yours?"

There was no point in arguing. In all fairness, Belle herself never felt the need to keep track of time in Belzerac, owing to the predictability that came with each sojourn, her departure so typically marked by the setting of the sun. She struggled to piece together her last memory — the descent of imminent nightfall in the Sapphire Forest. Yet in this beautiful landscape where they both now stood, there was nary the slightest hint of dusk. Could a day have already passed? How was it they both weren't back in Michelmont?

"Looks like it's just the two of us. No sign of the others," Julien said, glancing around. "I really don't understand any of this. It feels like a dream, and not a good one."

"Except dreams are rarely accompanied by music," she said, her thoughts drifting back to *Mélodie* once more. "This music is based on the legend of Orpheus and Eurydice. Do you know the story?"

He shook his head.

It was one of Belle's favorite Greek myths. "Orpheus and Eurydice are lovers. On the night of their wedding, Eurydice gets bitten by a snake and dies. Beside himself with grief, Orpheus travels to the Underworld to bring her back to the land of the living.

"He convinces Hades and Persephone — the King and Queen of the Underworld — to release her, and they agree on one condition: on their way back to the Upper World, Eurydice must walk behind

Orpheus and he is forbidden from looking at her."

"Sounds easy enough," shrugged Julien.

"You would think," Belle sighed, her eyes wistful. "Unfortunately, he is so overcome with passion that just as they reach the exit, he looks back."

"No kidding. What happens next?"

"Eurydice is immediately banished to the Underworld — this time for good. Devastated, Orpheus then spends the rest of his life roaming around Greece playing sad songs until he gets mauled to death by a group of drunken mad women."

"That sounds horrible. If only he hadn't looked back."

"But he had to. He couldn't help himself."

"Yes, he could. A little self-control never hurt anybody."

"Wouldn't be much of a story if he'd resisted the temptation and they made it back safely."

"That I concede."

Belle and Julien sat in silence. "We might as well look for the source of the music," she decided, after a long pause. "It doesn't sound far off from where we are."

Hand in hand, they ambled downhill until they arrived at the snaking banks of a glittering stream. In a shady glade sat an empty boat. Julien climbed in and grabbed hold of one of its oars.

"Come on," he said, "I think we need to get to the opposite side, where the music's coming from."

Is he serious? she wondered, hesitating. Meeting his gaze, she could have sworn she saw specks of gold in those stormy gray eyes.

Belle climbed in gingerly. It was her first time in a boat — the rickety wooden vessel tilted dramatically to the right, almost tipping over, and she hurriedly sat down, clutching the sides of the boat until it stabilized.

"Here," said Julien, passing her one of the two oars. "I'll paddle on the right and you do the left."

Traveling across when the current was flowing lengthways proved a little tricky but they soon got the hang of it and developed a working rhythm to their paddling strokes. The waters, a deep cerulean, glinted under the sun, and the flowery fragrance of lilacs which flanked both sides of the riverbanks grew heavier and more intoxicating. All this time, *Mélodie* continued to play.

Belle wasn't sure how long it took for them to reach the opposite bank, but when they finally did, her arms ached from all that rowing.

Leaves crunched underfoot as they disembarked and looked around. By now, the hems of her pajama pants were stained with blue mud from the earlier trek in the Sapphire Forest. Moreover, she was wet from all that sloshing about in the boat, though strangely, it didn't feel cold or chilly. Looking over, she saw that Julien's pajamas were soaked and clung heavily to him. He tried to shake off a few twigs that were snagged in his pants, but lost his footing and landed in a heap.

Belle giggled as she helped him to his feet. For that split second, thoughts of home were very far from both their minds. They had come this far and there was no turning back.

Continuing to follow the inviting trail of music, they soon arrived at a large cottage. It was constructed of stone ochres and had tall windows with bright blue shutters. Belle thought she might have painted a house like that once.

Moving closer, she and Julien saw that the door was left slightly ajar, as if visitors were expected. She looked at him nervously and he nodded. Julien gave it a gentle push and they stepped inside furtively.

The music was now more pronounced than ever, albeit more legato in style and languid in tempo. Belle's feet were still damp from the grass and moss, and they felt cold against the wood-panelled floors. But the lull of *Mélodie* was so enthralling she was determined to reach the source of it.

She scanned her surroundings. They had entered a sitting room, complete with richly upholstered armchairs set by a fireplace that was still going. In the middle of the room stood an oakwood coffee table adorned with... food!

Pastries, cakes, biscuits, and sandwiches were laid out nicely on fine porcelain plates. "Tea in Pajamas?" Julien teased. The aroma of freshly brewed coffee and tea wafted through the air and Belle inhaled deeply, beguiled by it all.

"You're late, Mademoiselle Belle," piped a deep, throaty voice.

It didn't sound like Julien. Spinning around, she was greeted by the sight of a tall brown fox, dressed smartly in a black dinner jacket and red bow tie. She peered over at Julien, whose face had gone quite white with fear. She soon saw why. Behind him with its feathered wings wrapped firmly around his shoulders was a human-sized nightingale, her chestnut feathers poking out from under a shiny black evening gown. The music had stopped.

"Who are you and how do you know my name?" Belle asked the fox.

He chuckled. "Pardon my ill manners, Mademoiselle. My name is François. And as to how I am acquainted with your good self, we make it a point to know everybody here."

"Where exactly is *here*?"

"Belzerac. You're still within the Sapphire Forest, just deeper in. You know, it stops looking blue beyond a certain point."

"Are you guys the ... Musicians?" Julien asked, his voice shaky.

"*Mais oui*, Monsieur Julien. *Enchanté*," said the nightingale, taking her wing off his shoulder and extending it for a friendly handshake.

He took it limply. "It's very nice to meet you too, Madame … er …"

"Nicole," she chirped. "Come on out, the rest of you, can't you see we have guests here?"

At her command, two other forest animals emerged from the rooms: a sleepy-eyed squirrel wearing a silky blouse, and a fluffy white rabbit decked in a formal suit. They were all dressed in black, Belle noticed.

"Simone." The squirrel curtsied.

"Raymond." The rabbit bowed.

"*Alors!*" exclaimed François the Fox, clasping his paws together in glee. "Now that we are all acquainted, what say we gather for a spot of tea?" He guided Belle and Julien to the sofa, gesturing for his guests to sit and eat.

The Musicians then took their places, picked up their instruments and started playing *Mélodie*. François led as the first violinist, Nicole the second, while Simone and Raymond played the viola and cello, respectively. It was a picture of perfect harmony.

Belle took a tiny bite of the apple danish set before her. The flaky pastry and tart filling melted in her mouth — it was simply the most divine thing she'd ever tasted. Next to her, Julien wasted no time devouring the éclairs and savory finger sandwiches. It wasn't long before the serving tray was emptied of its treats.

A sudden sense of fatigue washed over Belle. Her thoughts drifted back home to Michelmont and she wondered what her parents and brother were doing at that very moment.

"Wait a second," whispered Julien, his voice jolting her from her thoughts.

"Aren't the Musicians the bad guys? We should go."

They exchanged knowing glances, waiting for an opportune moment to make a swift exit.

But that was before the room started spinning.

The Grand Performance

Belle awoke to find herself lying in a large four-poster bed with creamy satin sheets. She blinked and looked around. She was alone.

"Julien?" she called out. No answer.

She got to her feet and tiptoed out of the bedroom and down the hallway. She stopped at the sitting room where they'd had tea and the Musicians had played the day before.

No one was there. All traces of cutlery and food had been cleared and the place looked spick and span. Bright rays of sunshine filtered through a semi-open window and she could hear the sound of birds chirping outside. It looked to be a glorious morning and she must have slept through the night.

"There you are!" The lilting sing-song voice of Nicole the Nightingale caught Belle offguard. She noticed that the bird was dressed in the same black dress as the day before. And as if reading Belle's mind, Nicole chirped, "Concert attire, my dear. Always ready to give a performance — that's what we do."

"Where's Julien? Was I asleep long?"

"All night, dear. He's prepping."

"Prepping for what?"

"You'll see. He's with the rest of your friends."

"My friends?" She realized that she was merely parroting — to a nightingale.

"Come with me," said Nicole.

Belle followed her down a steep flight of stairs into the basement. They walked past a long corridor of rooms until they reached two large, imposing doors at the very end. "Shhh ..." said the nightingale.

With a push, these opened into a grand concert hall, filled to capacity.

Belle could hardly believe what she saw. Never could she imagine that such a breathtakingly beautiful music theater might be tucked in the basement of a nondescript cottage in the woods. Its interiors were lavish – a dazzling crystal chandelier hung from the concert hall's frescoed ceiling and the place looked so impressively large that it could seat hundreds. Down many levels from the audience stood a long and wide stage, dimly lit and with its red velvet stage curtains still down.

"Where are my friends?" she turned to ask, but Nicole had disappeared.

"Ladies and gentlemen!" boomed a loud, imposing voice. It sounded familiar – where had she heard it before? Belle walked down many flights of steps past numerous aisles of seats. She strained to see who the speaker onstage was, and it didn't take her long to make out his pinkish skin and bumbling manner. It was Monsieur DuPorc!

She dashed down toward the stage, her bare feet thumping hard against the red-carpeted floor and her heart racing.

"May I present to you," he went on, "the Musicians, performing for us Gluck's *Mélodie*, accompanied by the Belzerac Symphony Orchestra."

Belle stopped at the foot of the stage, just as the stage curtains lifted. By this time, Monsieur DuPorc had retreated from sight.

"You're blocking us!" shouted an audience member from behind her. She backed away to the nearest corner, stooping low and straining for a good view.

Mélodie began. The Musicians took center stage, and the rest of her friends were part of the orchestra. Cheesy Bear was playing the oboe, while the DuPorcs were on flute and clarinet. And, in an inconspicuous corner of the brass section stood Julien holding the French horn. Everyone looked focused and serious.

She thought of yelling but that seemed out of place in a setting like this so she stayed where she was, afraid to take her eyes off the stage lest they disappeared from her sight.

The performance was mesmerizing. How was it her friends could play these instruments and so well? Had they been here and practicing the whole time? Is this where all the missing Belzeracians were — in the orchestra?

The piece soon came to an end and the lights went out. The audience applauded enthusiastically and Belle clapped along, wondering what might happen next.

Then with a dramatic bang, the lights came on again, but this time, the spotlight was no longer on the Musicians. They had, it seemed, retreated into the shadows with the rest of the orchestra. Instead, it shone on a solitary figure in a white cotton nightdress – a girl of her age with unmistakable raven hair and a blue headband.

The girl opened her mouth, warbling the vocal solo of *Mélodie* as the instruments accompanied softly in the background.

"*TESS!*"

Belle's cry echoed throughout the concert hall, startling everyone. The girl onstage went quiet. All music grounded to a halt.

Nothing held Belle back now as she scampered onstage, running to her best friend and flinging herself into her arms. "Tess, where have you been? I've been looking all over for you!"

When they finally pulled away, Tess's eyes were downcast.

"Come on, Tess, let's go home!"

A pause. "We — we can't," she said softly.

"What do you mean we can't?" Belle asked, incredulous.

All the lights came on. The audience remained seated, now watching a live show of another sort, but no one seemed to be complaining. Perhaps they were relieved not to have to hear *Mélodie* played over and over again. Belle knew she certainly was.

Julien stepped forward, still clutching his French horn. "Belle, I know it sounds odd, but we can't go home yet," he began. "Not until the Musicians are able to play something different. All this time, they've been practicing and recruiting more new members into their orchestra in the hopes of achieving a different sound."

"But despite the many interpretations and arrangements and renditions of *Mélodie*, it's still the exact same tune," Tess continued. "It's kept us all locked in this weird zone."

"I don't understand," said Belle. "What does any of this have to do with us?" She was truly confounded.

Finally, François spoke up. "If you must know, *ma chérie*, it's because of *you* that we're all here."

There was a long pause in the concert hall.

"Tea in Pajamas, does that ring a bell?" the fox went on. "Your crossing over into our world has created a kind of misalignment in time and space. We were playing *Mélodie* one particular Wednesday afternoon when Tess appeared at our home."

Belle stopped to think. So all this confusion must have been the result of a miscalculation on her part or Tess's when they'd each had tea in their pajamas. That might explain why she herself had arrived at the pie-making competition in Belzerac while Tess ended up in the Sapphire Forest with the Musicians.

"And she gave us quite a scare too," Raymond the Rabbit interjected. "Never before had we seen anyone from where you come from. But we welcomed Tess all the same. We performed for her, and it was then that we realized —"

"Let me show you," said Simone the Squirrel, chiming in. She picked up her viola and played *Mélodie*. "Look at my fingers. I'm playing scales. G major. Yet all that comes out is *Mélodie*. It's the same for the rest of our quartet. Since Tess arrived, we haven't managed to play anything else."

"Is that why you keep repeating this piece?" Belle asked. "Suppose someone came along and played something different, might that free us from this predicament?"

"That's a theory we've been trying to prove," said François. "Though obviously none of us here has been successful thus far."

Belle's eyes darted across to a far corner of the stage where a grand piano sat

— it was worth a try. She attempted to recall those music lessons she'd had when younger, but she was uncertain if she could presently even manage a simple tune. She walked over to the piano and sat down.

The stool squeaked slightly and she discovered that, unlike before, her feet could now effortlessly reach the pedals below. Her fingers rested limply on the cold, ivory keys. For all her past protests that music had to be spontaneous, she was now feeling anything but.

Searching her surroundings for inspiration, an image entered Belle's mind — that window in her music room by which her piano sat. Through those glass panes, she had witnessed her first sunset, rainbow, thunderstorm, and falling snow. Gazing out of it was like stealing a glimpse into her own heart. The scenes outside often evoked feelings of love, longing, joy, wonder, and awe — feelings she would transpose into music.

Belle pictured herself peering through that same window once more, and imagined what it might look like in that very moment. Autumn was approaching, and soon the grass in her garden would be blanketed by fallen leaves. She saw herself lying flat on the ground, her auburn hair disappearing into the coppery carpet. She could almost catch a whiff of her mother's cooking — the homely smells of dinner wafting from the kitchen. Her father and brother would be chatting nearby, their voices indistinct.

Her thoughts had drifted so far she scarcely realized she had started playing. Belle's hands were dancing across the octaves and her fingers gliding across the piano keys. Andante and arpeggios, chords and crescendos. And the melodies that spilled out ... weren't *Mélodie*.

The Two Doors

*S*he didn't know what or how long she had been playing but when Belle finally lifted her fingers to look down at the keys, she only saw her hands. The piano had disappeared, and with it, the concert hall and the Musicians. Everything was looking very blue again, she saw, for they were back in the middle of the Sapphire Forest.

"You did it!" Tess exclaimed, as she huddled around Belle with the rest of her friends.

Belle looked around and saw the happy faces of Julien, Cheesy Bear, and the DuPorcs, evidently relieved to be a step closer to home, wherever that was.

Mélodie was no more, and in its place, she could now hear the hum of insects and the rustle of leaves. She had done it somehow – produced a different tune — although she remained unsure how that happened. Before this, she'd never dreamed she could accomplish something others couldn't, and this newfound knowledge made her feel strangely alive — and free.

At the same time, Belle found herself feeling somewhat disappointed that what she had managed to achieve in the concert hall was not yet enough to get her home. Having been away from Michelmont for so long, she sorely missed her parents, her brother Éric, her school, and her heretofore "boring" old life.

The group now readied itself for the trek out of the Sapphire Forest, with Julien leading the way. To think this was the same spiky-haired new friend from school who had, not too long ago, asked to sit at her lunch table.

"How are you doing?" Belle asked, running to catch up with him. Up until then, he hadn't complained, but she could sense he was exhausted and, like her, missing home.

"I'm doing great," he said, with a nervous laugh. Maybe it was the blue light but in that instant, "Julien Hedgehog" looked rather handsome. "It's been a pleasure escorting you on this adventure," he continued. "When I moved to Michelmont, I knew there'd be new experiences waiting, but this I could never have imagined. I guess I should even say thanks."

Belle sighed. "Don't be silly. This whole Tea in Pajamas business, it was selfish of me," she said. "I was bored and I thought life here was so much better. I'm so sorry I dragged you into this."

"Well, let's just focus on getting ourselves out of here before dark," Julien said, helping her across a muddy puddle.

He was right. They had a mission, and there wasn't a point in feeling sorry for herself. Belle trudged resolutely ahead.

As they approached a small clearing, Julien suddenly stopped in his tracks. A smile crept onto his face. "Check us out," he said.

Belle looked down at her hands and feet and saw that they weren't blue anymore. Neither were her striped cotton pajamas and most evidently, her hair, which had regained its fiery shade of red. Monsieur DuPorc and his wife looked very pink and Cheesy Bear's fur was back to its deep chocolate brown.

"Wow," said Tess, examining her surroundings in awe. "I feel like Dorothy who just landed back in the colorful Land of Oz."

Belle smiled at the reference, a most apt one, except she had no ruby slippers to click her heels in and chime: *There's no place like home.* If only it were that simple.

The DuPorcs and Cheesy Bear, who had ventured several steps ahead, were stooped low and closely examining the ground, which looked very unusually shiny. The rest of them hurried forth for a better look. A blanket of golden leaves was glittering resplendently under the sunlight, leaving everyone awestruck and captivated.

"I don't remember seeing all this on the way in — do you?" Belle asked. They all shook their heads.

"Wow," said Cheesy Bear abruptly, "you should all ... umm ... look up." He was on his feet and gazing upward, all agog.

Lifting their heads, they saw *him*. Bathed in a majestic golden glow, Monsieur L'Arbre rose head and shoulders above all other trees in the Sapphire Forest. His trunk was embellished by an intricate maze of leaves, creepers, and hanging roots, which danced to the wind like tassels on a gypsy's costume.

"We've found him," whispered Monsieur DuPorc to his nodding wife.

Belle waited for the magnificent tree to speak, but he only gestured in regal, elegant movements of his strong, sturdy branches. She watched, mesmerized. With leaves falling around her in a golden cascade, Belle suddenly felt engulfed in a sense of calm and stillness she had never before known.

It seemed Monsieur L'Arbre knew why they had come. He stiffened, as if signaling for all to move aside. Belle and her friends took several steps back, bracing themselves for the big reveal.

From that point, everything happened quickly. Hanging vines and overgrowth that had previously obscured his trunk were lifting like giant curtains before them. And with a thunderous clap, two enormous golden doors rose swiftly to the surface of his trunk. They had no knobs on them.

"Maybe we should knock," suggested Tess.

Cheesy Bear and Monsieur DuPorc approached the gilded doors, but Belle stepped in their way. "Let me," she said. "I got everyone here and I should be the one to bring us back home."

They nodded and stepped back.

Now the question was: which door should she knock on first? They were so huge and widely spaced apart that Belle couldn't possibly reach for both at once. She decided to try the one to the left.

With a deafening creak, it swung open. Everyone edged forward for a better look: it was a scene she recognized immediately — the pie-making competition in Belzerac.

Belle's heart sank — she had hoped to see her dining table back in Michelmont. But evidently, it was not yet her turn to go home.

She turned to Cheesy Bear and the DuPorcs. "I guess this is goodbye, then."

She didn't know if she would see them the following Wednesday or ever again. Tea in Pajamas had come to be a central part of her life, but it also felt like that journey had come full circle. Perhaps it was time to let go of Belzerac and everyone in it, and it seemed they understood this too.

"Everything's going to be all right," said Cheesy, hugging her tenderly. "You are a wonderful person, don't you forget it."

"Know that you are very loved, because that's all that matters," added Monsieur DuPorc.

It wasn't the typical "we'll miss you" speech she was expecting but maybe this was the best advice to give anyone. She blinked away tears as they broke apart.

As Cheesy Bear and the DuPorcs disappeared through the open door, it shut firmly after them. Once again, vines and creepers descended to conceal it completely. Now only the other door remained.

"If you don't mind," Belle said to Tess and Julien, who were standing behind her, misty-eyed, "I'd like to do the honors too for the other door."

They nodded and stepped aside.

Belle approached the golden portal with trepidation. This would be her last chance. It was gleaming so brightly she could see her own reflection staring back at her — a tired but determined little girl, barefoot and in her pajamas. She knocked on it once.

Nothing happened.

She tried again, more forcefully.

She went on knocking for a third, fourth, fifth, and sixth time.

Still nothing.

"Perhaps you need to say something," Tess suggested. "You know how Dorothy does the no-place-like-home speech to get back to Kansas?"

"But what do I say?"

Nobody had an answer.

"Please open up. We'd like to go home," she called out in earnest.

The door remained shut.

"There's no place like home!"

Clearly, this wasn't the Land of Oz, and that line had no effect whatsoever. Belle was getting exasperated.

After several more futile attempts, she sank to the ground, crestfallen. She had done everything in her power to get home, but now, it seemed, all had come to naught.

"Although I don't want it to end this way, I accept responsibility for all of this," Belle said, looking up at Monsieur L'Arbre and addressing him. "I concede that I took Tea in Pajamas too far and lost sight of home— of reality.

"The irony is … after having gone through one heck of an extraordinary adventure in Belzerac, I've come to appreciate just what 'extraordinary' means to me. It's my most ordinary life in Michelmont.

"Now my dear friends are implicated in this mess of my own making, yet they have been nothing but gracious and sympathetic through it all. Tess and Julien deserve to go home and get on with their lives.

"With Belzerac, I thought I'd discovered a place so magical and wonderful. I was obsessed with Wednesday afternoons, and so afraid my time in Belzerac might disappear if I turned my attention away from it, even if only for a moment.

"So Tea in Pajamas took on a life of its own. It never occured to me that I'd have any trouble getting home ... home, which I'd taken for granted. Now here we are, lost, on the cusp of finding our way back ... yet ... not quite.

"Monsieur L'Arbre, please will you show us the way home? We're all quite ready to get out of our pajamas, put on some shoes, and do something else next Wednesday afternoon. As for me, I want to be around to tell my family just how much I love them."

"THE DOOR!" cried Tess excitedly. "IT'S OPENING!"

Indeed it was. Belle got to her feet, staring as the portal, which only moments ago had been sealed shut, unbolted with a deafening quake. From it emerged bright rays of light that spread out like giant fingers.

It was the evening sun of Michelmont spilling through her kitchen window. In the middle stood the table where she always took her tea, and on it sat an empty plate and teacup. She saw the dining chair that was not pushed back in and the flaky pastry crumbs that were scattered on the floor beneath. The scene was exactly the way she had left it.

The sun was setting. *I could be home for dinner*, she thought, her heart so full of joy she thought it might burst.

Hand in hand, the children ran, their every step taking them further from Belzerac and closer to Michelmont.

As they crossed the threshold, Belle heard the familiar lull of *Mélodie*. The music was so stirring, and she was tempted to glance behind her, but somehow, the tale of Orpheus and Eurydice came to mind.

"No matter what," Belle said to her friends, "don't look back."

END

Author's Note

There was once a girl who struggled with disordered behaviors. She fought long and hard in a battle she thought she might never emerge victorious from, and searched far and wide for a key that might unlock her from her unfreedoms. Not knowing at first where to look, she spent much time researching for a cure. Eventually, however, she came to realize that the exact tools she sought for this purpose lay deep within her. They were discernment and self-awareness.

That girl was me.

This book is an allegorical representation of my little inward journey toward a place of honesty and truth — one that is ongoing.

For a time, I had thought about writing a long, detailed account of this challenging period, and perhaps one day I will. However, the idea of "coming home to myself" was also essentially about being reacquainted with that child in me, and I have always wanted to write a children's book, especially one that might connect with readers on a deeper level. That is how *Tea in Pajamas* came about.

I would like to thank my family and friends who supported this passion project of mine, particularly my loving and talented husband Joseph who provided the illustrations to this book. I'm also grateful to Melvin Neo, Mindy Pang, Anita Teo and She-reen Wong at Marshall Cavendish who were patient and encouraging throughout the entire publication process. And finally, my utmost gratitude is reserved for the One who loves me unconditionally and gifted me with this precious life.

Tea in Pajamas is a story of hope: of a life that is beautiful and inspiring when seen through the eyes of a child—and with a discerning heart.

With that, it is my sincere hope that you enjoy Belle's little tale of discernment and self-awareness.

Belle's adventures continue in

Tea in Pajamas:

Beyond Belzerac

Six o'clock in evening was an odd time for the house to be empty. It was now a full hour since Belle Marie came home, showered, and chucked her dirty laundry in the washing machine. The soles of her feet were grazed with tiny cuts and callused, and her striped cotton pajamas – filthy, ragged, and battle-weary – had certainly seen better days.

Belle was desperate to see her family, but upon her return to Michelmont, there was no sign of her parents or older brother

Éric. It was a little late for a grocery run, but seeing how Mom's car wasn't in the driveway, her mother and brother must've made a highly unusual decision to get takeout for dinner. And while it wasn't uncommon for Dad to still be at work at this hour, she found it difficult to tamp down a gnawing anxiety that things weren't quite right.

The kitchen bore no trace of activity. No meat was left to thaw on the counter, the cutting board was devoid of its usual carrots and onions, and the slow cooker – typically switched on almost all day – was not even plugged into the power socket, its contents dry and empty.

Was this home?

As far as Belle was aware, it certainly looked the part. The house was exactly the way she'd left it, yet that once distinct sense of warmth and ease that came with being home was markedly absent. The place was spick and span, and fixtures and furnishings were in their rightful place, yet an unmistakable lackadaisical quality clung to the air. Why did home feel so grim and somber?

A gust of wind blew in from an open window, making Belle shiver. She pulled the hood of her gray fleece jacket over her head and tucked her hands into the pockets of her blue jeans. Autumn was in full swing and the days were getting shorter: with nightfall imminent, she noted with irony how in a few hours she'd be back in pajamas, and found herself repulsed by the thought.

No thanks, but I'll sleep in my jeans if I have to, she resolved. After a longer-than-planned sojourn in Belzerac, Tea in Pajamas was a chapter she'd closed – at least for now.

So where was everybody?

Rachel Tey is an editorial consultant. She lives in Singapore with her husband and two children. *Tea in Pajamas* is her debut novel, the first in a multi-part series. Look out for its sequel, *Tea in Pajamas: Beyond Belzerac*, where the adventures of Belle, Tess, and Julien continue.

Visit www.racheltey.com or connect with her on social media for all the latest updates.